Author's Note

In January 2006, I spent three inspiring and unforgettable days in the oncology department at the Schneider Children's Medical Center of Israel, conducting workshop sessions with children and teenagers who were sick with cancer. The workshop was called "Drawing with Objects." The kids created self-portraits and portraits of their families using objects found in everyday life, as well as items from the hospital. The pictures made by the younger children appear—with many thanks—on the endpapers. This book is dedicated to them.

SCHWARTZ & WADE BOOKS and colophon are
trademarks of Random House, Inc.

www.randomhouse.com/kids

Educators and librarians, for a variety of teaching tools, visit us at
www.randomhouse.com/teachers

Library of Congress Cataloging-in-Publication Data

Piven, Hanoch.
My dog is as smelly as dirty socks: and other funny family portraits/Hanoch Piven.—1st ed.
p. cm.
Summary: A young girl draws a family portrait, then makes it more accurate by adding common objects to show aspects of each member's personality, such as her father's playfulness, her mother's sweetness, and her brother's strength.
ISBN: 978-0-375-84052-4 (tr.) — ISBN: 978-0-375-94052-1 (lib. bdg.)
[1. Portraits–Fiction. 2. Individuality–Fiction. 3. Family life–Fiction.] I. Title.

PZ7.P68943My 2007
[E]–dc22
2006021936

The text of this book is set in Apollo.
The illustrations are rendered in gouache
on watercolor adorned with glued-on objects.

PRINTED IN CHINA

10 9 8 7 6 5 4 3

First Edition

My Dog is as Smelly as Dirty Socks

AND OTHER FUNNY FAMILY PORTRAITS
BY HANOCH PIVEN

schwartz & wade books • new york

MY DADDY   MY

MY BiG   MOMMY

BROTHER

MY BABY BROTHER

My teacher asked
me to draw a picture
of my family, and
this is what I drew.

I showed it to her
and she said,
**"How great
is that!"**

But I didn't like it.

Look at my dad.

There are so many things
about him that you don't
see in this picture.

Like . . .

My daddy is as
jumpy as a SPRING

and as playful as a
SPINNING TOP.

He is as fun as a
PARTY FAVOR.

But sometimes he's as stubborn
as a KNOT in a ROPE.

So I made my
picture better, see?

That's *him*!

(Isn't he nutty?)

And what about
this drawing of
my mom?

Sorry, but it doesn't
tell the whole story.

My mommy is as soft
as the softest FLUFF

and as bright as
the brightest LIGHT.

She is as tasty as the
crunchiest COOKIE.

No, TASTIER!
She's as delicious
as a CROISSANT.

That's my
yummy mommy!

(Mommy, I'm going to eat you all up.)

And now you're probably wondering what my big brother is *really* like.

Well...

My brother is as amusing as a game of MARBLES

and as strong as a BASEBALL BAT,

but when we play hide-and-seek, he's as sneaky as a SNAKE.

Oh, and one more thing:
He eats like a . . .

(I'll give you a clue: "Oink, oink.")

. . . PIG!

That's my brother
right there.

And what about
my baby brother?

He is not this quiet.

My baby brother is as sweet as CANDY (this is true).

But he never stops crying!

 He's as loud as a WHISTLE,

or maybe a HORN,

 or even an ALARM CLOCK.

No, LOUDER! He's as loud as a FIRE TRUCK.

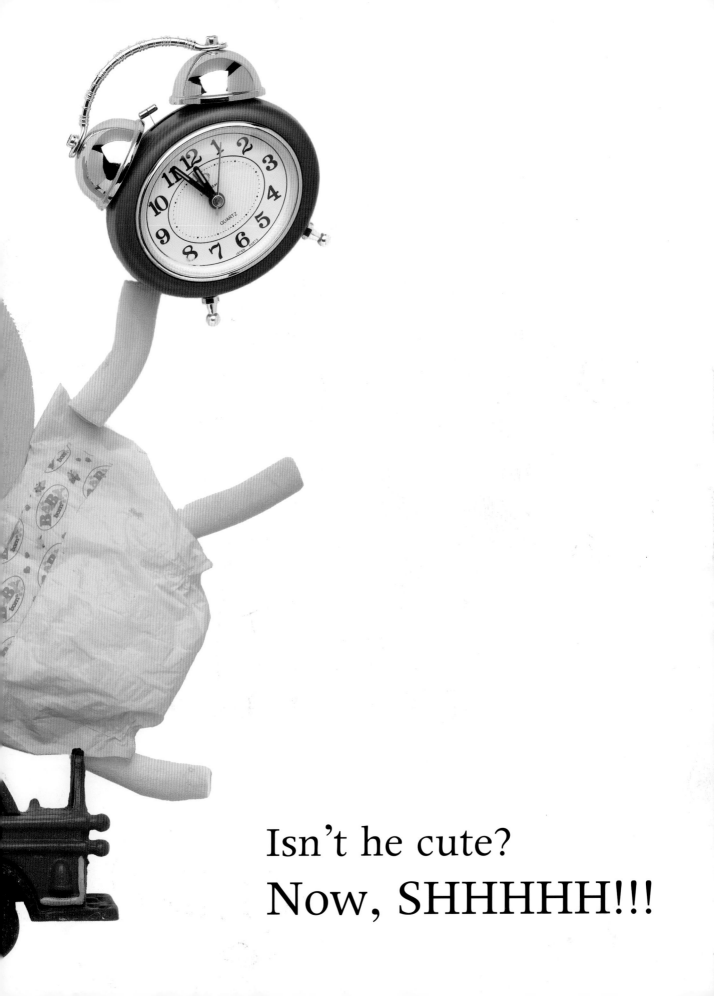

Isn't he cute?
Now, SHHHHH!!!

And then there
is Schmutz.

I'll be honest with you . . .
Schmutz stinks!

Schmutz is as stinky
as an ONION.

He's as nasty
as canned FISH,

as icky as PEPPERONI,

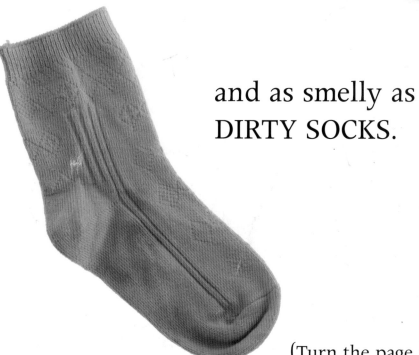

and as smelly as
DIRTY SOCKS.

(Turn the page at your own risk. . . .)

YUCKY-BOO!

(I warned you.)

But what about me?

Well, there is
SOOOOOOOOO
much I want to tell you
about me!

I am a princess,

as majestic as a CROWN

 and as sugary as a JELLY BEAN.

I am as sharp as a PENCIL

 and as sparkly as a STAR.

(Wait—I have more!)

I am as colorful as a FLOWER

and as lovely as PERFUME.

 I am as strong as a STONE

and as good as an ANGEL.

(Hey! I'm not done yet.)

I am as funny as a tickly FEATHER

 and as curious as
a MAGNIFYING GLASS.

I am faster than a CALCULATOR

 and all around, as special as
BEACH GLASS.

But more important than all of that . . .

My heart is BIG...

and with it,
I love my special
family.

Now tell me about *your* special family. What do they look like?

Here's a list of objects that can help you think about how to make portraits of your family:

Things that say "smart":
ruler, numbers, owl

Things that say "funny":
chattering teeth, clown nose, toy monkey

Things that say "scratchy":
steel wool, sharp teeth, cactus

Things that say "soft":
teddy bear, cotton ball, slipper

Things that say "strong":
action figure, elephant, hammer